BREATHE ME TO LIFE

JOLANTHE ALEKSANDER

This novel is a work of fiction. Any resemblance to actual persons, living or deceased is coincidental. The characters, names, plots, or incidents within are the product of the author's imagination. References to actual events or locations are included to give the fiction a sense of reality.

Copyright 2018, Jolanthe Aleksander

All rights reserved. No part of this book may be reproduced, stored, or transmitted in any form, by any means, without written consent from Jolanthe Aleksander.

Cover Design: SelfPubBookCovers.com/Ravenborn

Cover Design: Tell Tale Book Covers

Typography: Funky Book Designs

Published by: Eclectic Bard Books

ACKNOWLEDGEMENTS & DEDICATION

No successful project is completed without the help of others. I want to send a great big Thank You to Darlene and Andi for being my sounding boards. I'd also like to send out another great big Thank You to Kelli for your inspirational words.

To all the princesses and princes who have lost hope that there is the "one" out there for you. Straighten your crowns, get out there, and go look for them. They're directionally challenged and got lost.

I hope you never stopped believing in the possibility of a Happily Ever After.

Happy Reading!

CHAPTER 1

*S*even Years Ago

*H*olding her breath, Ailsa quietly stood by her closed bedroom door. Her ear pressed against the cool wood, she listened for any sound of stirring of any members of her latest and last foster family. She only had a few more months until she aged out of the system. Her freedom was within reach, but being patient was turning out to be a challenge.

Not a single sound came from the other side of the door. Ailsa's eyes darted to the corner of the small room and landed on a ladder back chair. Hurriedly, she pulled away from the door, crossed the short distance to reach the chair, grabbed it, and wedged it beneath the doorknob. Funny enough, she never once sat on its age-worn seat. If truth be told, she hadn't trusted it to hold her weight. She sent up a petition to the Goddess begging that it didn't fall apart should one of her foster parents wake and decide to check on their willful ward.

Crossing the carpeted floor, Ailsa stood between the threadbare, flowered sheets that served as curtains. Playfully, they danced on the current of the wind coming through the open window. The new moon, glowing brightly against the blue-black canvas of the sky, shone a path of white light to the grove of trees just beyond the manicured back yard, It beckoned her to walk its trail, to heed the call of the music that whispered to her heart and soul.

Before she could second-guess herself, she threw one leg over the window ledge, followed by the other. Not for the first time, she found herself happy they had put her in the first floor room off to the side of the large kitchen as she dropped the short distance to the ground.

Kneeling down, she sucked in a breath as the cool wind brushed against her face. She looked over her shoulder, half-expecting to find someone staring out the window down at her, and then she took off running. The grass, still damp from the early evening rain, was cool beneath her bare feet. The hem of her thin flannel nightgown, dampened by the moisture-ridden blades, clung to her ankles, threatening to trip her. Still she ran on. The risk of discovery before she reached the glade goaded her on, spurring her feet to a greater speed. She wove her way through the trees with an urgency she didn't fully understand, but heeded nonetheless.

Finally, she was deep in the forest and out of sight of the house. One hand kneaded her side muscles rubbing out a cramp, while the other clutched a tree. The bark rough against her palm, she bent over to catch her breath. She inhaled the earthy scent of the woods and soil, the mustiness of fallen leaves decaying on the ground. Head bent down, she closed her eyes and let the music that drew her here, wash over her. Straightening, Ailsa took a deep breath and pushed away from the tree. Following the music, she laughed and thought of the Pied Piper of Hamelin. *Am I like the mice blindly following the music to meet their doom, or the children who were taken until their parents had learned the lesson of going back on their word,* she wondered. *Does it matter?* She didn't think so. There was no one to miss her.

Coming to a stop at the edge of trees circling the meadow, her mouth gaped in awe at the sight that greeted her eyes, and the music that led her there ceased.

~

*K*ellan, Prince of the Light Court, searched the area for the reason the revelry had come to an abrupt halt. His gaze fell on the waif-like creature that had crossed through the thinned veil into Faerie. Rising to his feet, he brushed off the delicate, grasping hand of Devany from his arm. Without regard to her gasp of offence, or sparing her a second thought, he wove his way through the glittering throng of Fae to reach the female.

Out of the corner of his eye, he caught the sight of Prince Orin also heading towards the chit. That wouldn't do at all. There was no way he would allow a lesser Prince, with his pale skin and equally pale hair and eyes, to lay claim on a prize he had decided was his. Possessiveness had never been one of his vices, but feeling it firsthand but didn't halt his quick steps or diminish his determination.

It had been a long time since a female had sparked Kellan's interest for more than immediate satisfaction of having his carnal needs met. He may have scratched the itch, but the desire to spend more time with the insipid females was fleeting. Their sole focus was climbing their way to a seat that much closer to the throne than the one they currently occupied. Not even Devany, with her golden beauty, enticed him to bond with her.

She wasn't a full blood mortal, of that he was sure. He could sense Fae blood coursing through her veins. She was shabbily dressed in a gown that had seen better days and would have served its purpose better as a rag. Her dark hair, with its streaks of auburn glowing in the light of the bonfire, tumbled down her back in a riot of curls, brushing the curve of her waist. She was young, by Fae and mortal standards, yet her luminescent skin, big green eyes, and high cheekbones hinted at the exquisite beauty yet to be.

He reached her just before Orin did. He swallowed a chuckle as the lesser Prince bowed and backed away, muttering his displeasure at being thwarted under his breath. He turned his attention to the girl staring up at him in wonder and amazement. Smiling, Kellan cocked his head to the side, "And who might you be?"

Her cheeks flushed pink. The tip of her tongue darted out, moistening her lips, "Uuuum...hi." She raised a hand in greeting.

Kellan arched a brow in amusement. "UmHi. What an unusual name."

"What? No," she shook her head, "sorry, my name is Ailsa. You're beautiful," she blurted out. She turned her head and covered her mouth with her hand in dismay.

Gently cupping the side of her face, Kellan turned her face back to him and smiled, "'Tis pleased I am that you find me so. A male likes to know when a female finds his form appealing, especially as lovely a female as yourself." Stepping back, he lowered his hand and gave her a small bow of his head. "You have gifted me with the giving of your name. Shall I do the same for you, Ailsa?" His voice surrounded her like a warm embrace. The timbre and lilt of it were a symphony to her ears, one she was sure she would never tire of listening to.

She stared up into his eyes. They were a vibrant blue with shards of gold darting toward the pupils and twinkled with amusement. Realizing she'd been caught staring again, embarrassment flushed her cheeks as she belatedly answered his question, "Yes, please."

"You may call me Kellan." A tingle raced up her spine as he

took her hand, raised it to his mouth, and pressed his lips to the back of her fingers.

For the first time since Kellan stepped in her view, the tittering from those who were also in the glen reached her ears. Her eyes scanned over the crowd in the glittering clothes then down at what she wore. She shouldn't have come, no matter how much the music had pulled her. Embarrassment of another kind had her turning to leave only to halted by Kellan stepping in front of her.

"You're not leaving so soon, are you?"

Ailsa stole a quick glance over her shoulder, "I'm not really dressed for a party." She tucked an errant strand of hair behind her ear, "I'm sorry I interrupted your celebration. I shouldn't have come."

Looking down at her, Kellan cocked his head to the side. "Why did you come? What brought you out on a night such as this?"

Fighting to keep from squirming under his intense regard, she balled her hands into fists, the edges of her fingernails biting into her palms. "I heard the music."

"Did you indeed? And you decided to leave the comfort of your bed to find where the music came from?" He picked up her hand, tucked it in the crook of his arm, and turned to lead her towards the people standing around in their finery, the likes of which she had never seen.

"Yes," she confirmed, frowning when she tugged on her hand only to find it tightly locked in his grasp. "Stop." Ailsa planted her feet in an attempt to pull him to a standstill, only to stumble. His quick reflexes saved her from kissing the ground as he pulled her snug against his side. Her heart racing, she breathed in his scent and soaked up his warmth. Snickers and comments from the crowd reached her ears. Hanging her head, she pushed away from him. "Sorry, I have to go."

"Do you not wish to dance?" He asked, stopping her flight.

She did want to dance. She wanted to be carried away by the music that had drawn her to the glen in the first place. She wanted to bask in the light of the full moon that seemed to glow brighter here. If she were honest with herself, she wanted to enjoy Kellan's company a little while longer. He made her nervous, but he also made her feel safe. She found that combination frightening, intoxicating, and addictive. There was one little problem though. "Uuuum...well, there's no music."

One corner of his mouth quirked, "You've made an excellent point." A wave of his hand and music, once again, filled the air.

Throwing her head back, Ailsa laughed as Kellan spun her around. Her feet flew over the thick carpet of the grass, never stopping, never stumbling. For the first time, she felt graceful. Beneath his gaze, she felt beautiful.

Long into the night, they danced. Soon she forgot how out of place she felt. Ailsa laughed freely for the first time since she was a small child. She felt free and thought nothing of her appearance or the quality of the clothing she wore, nor did anyone call attention to them.

The festivities dissipated and the revelers settled beneath a canopy of trees to feast and drink. She grasped on to the thread of happiness rising up in her, desperate to remember the feeling. Sitting on the pillow Kellan had led her to before being called away, Ailsa took a deep breath and raised her eyes up to the sparkling lights flittering overhead.

CHAPTER 2

"You do know you're nothing but a curiosity to him, don't you?"

Tearing her gaze from the twinkling lights, Ailsa turned her head towards the velvet, smooth voice. A man with hair the color of corn silk and eyes a pale sage, stood looking down his patrician nose at her. She noticed him when she had first spoken to Kellan. He had, for some reason, bowed and walked away. She had also spotted him standing on the outer edges of where the dancing had taken place talking with a svelte blonde woman.

"Excuse me, do I know you?"

Chuckling he knelt down, "Of course you don't know me, you silly child. You don't know anyone here. Not even the Prince."

"What prince?"

"Oh, this is just too rich," the stranger stated, reaching out to flip a length of her hair over her shoulder, "that should tell you something right there."

Ailsa shrank from his touch, the guard she'd previously let down was now fully reinstated. "I really don't know what you're talking about," she replied, her voice quivering.

"And that, dear girl, is exactly my point. The male you have spent the evening with sees you as nothing but a plaything. He thinks so little of you that he hasn't even told you his name."

"But he has," she protested. "He said his name is Kellan."

"Yes, but did he tell you he was Prince Kellan of the Summer Court?" he asked, smugly.

Ailsa cocked her head to the side and squinted her eyes, "How do I know you're telling the truth?"

"I have no need to lie," he huffed, indignation coating his words. "Don't get me wrong, I can stretch and twist my words to not resemble the truth, but I don't lie."

"And he does?"

"Omission of all the facts is an unspoken lie in of itself. Is it not?"

Closing her eyes, Ailsa turned her head, wanting to shut out his words. She couldn't deny that she'd often thought the same thing about lies of omission. There had to be a reason Kellan didn't tell her he was a prince. It wasn't like they were in a committed relationship or really knew each other. They had just met after all. Still, for some reason the lapse in disclosing his title stung. And what was it to this stranger? What did he get out of telling on Kellan? "You sure do have a lot to say against Kellan, but you haven't told me your name either."

He chuckled, "Introductions require looking at each other."

Rolling her eyes beneath her closed lids, Ailsa sighed and opened them as she turned her face back towards him. "You were saying?" She met his silver-green eyes. There was nothing friendly or warm about them.

"You amuse me," he stated, "and that's a good thing for you."

"Really? Why?"

"Because if you didn't I would strike you where you sit," he declared with a sneer. "Your youth and ignorance along with the fact that you amuse me, buy you a little lee-way. And by little, I mean you a nearing the edge of my tolerance of your insolence."

Ailsa pushed herself up from her seat, "As lovely as this has been, I think it's time for me to go."

"Not so fast," he rose from his kneeling position, "Introductions still need to be made."

"No, really. That's alright. You needn't bother."

"No bother at all," he countered, stepping in front on her as she moved to escape, "I did, after all, say I would give you my name, Ailsa."

"How do you know my name?" she asked, craning her neck to look up at him. How had she not notice how tall he was or how tall Kellan was for that matter?

"I have extremely good hearing. Shall we get these formalities over with?"

Ailsa could hear the impatience lacing his voice. What choice did she have? The sooner he told her his name, which he seemed to think was of great importance, the sooner she could get back to the house. She needed to get back before anyone discovered her absence. "Fine, let's do this," she agreed with impatience of her own. She plastered the practiced smile she usually saved for people she didn't like and fought the urge to roll her eyes, which was harder and hurt more than she ever thought it would, when he glared down at her.

"My name, you impertinent chit, is Prince Orin of the Spring Court."

"Good to know. Can I go now?"

"Oh, but you haven't had any refreshments yet."

"That's okay. I can get something when I get home."

"That won't due at all." He stared over her shoulder, "Even now, Prince Kellan quenches his thirst in the company of another."

Turning, she looked in the direction Orin indicated. A touch of jealousy flared within her at seeing the lithe blonde, who with her cornflower blue eyes had shot daggers at her all evening, press her body against Kellan's side while her hand reached out to snag a goblet from his. The fact that the expression on his face was one of irritation did little to assuage the unfamiliar feeling running through her. Facing Orin again, "Manners say it would be rude of me to not accept your offer," she stated before her better sense of self-preservation could halt the words in their tract.

"Indeed," he responded with a smirk. "Shall we?" he asked holding out his arm.

Ailsa stood, rooted to her spot. *Nice going, idiot,* she mentally scolded herself, *You couldn't just thank him for his offer and go, could you? You just had to go and get jealous over a man you only met hours ago. Well, you put your foot in your mouth now, you better not keep his royal pain in the ass waiting.*

CHAPTER 3

Prince Orin had escorted her to the opposite side of the glen where those eating, drinking, and engaging in other activities lounged. Overlaying the sounds of the night creatures singing their songs, were the noises of voices raised in talk and laughter, glass goblets clinking against each other, and the carnal grunts and moans that came of bodies joining together in a dance as old as time. She tried hard not to stare with limited success. Ailsa couldn't stop her cheeks from blushing any more than she could the looks of amusement from lighting up the faces of the participants when she had been caught watching a little too long. Orin had left her standing beneath an oak with the promise to come back. Truthfully, she wouldn't mind if he too found himself otherwise occupied.

"There you are," Kellan announced, startling her.

"Here I am," she agreed, bowing her head and refusing to look him in the eye, in case he saw evidence of her jealousy.

"Why did you not stay where I left you?"

"Well, I did, for a long time too, I might add, and then Prince Orin insisted I have some refreshments before I go. So why didn't you tell me you were some kind of prince or something?"

Tucking a finger beneath her chin, Kellan raised her face and peered into her eyes, "Because in this time and place, titles are meaningless."

"What do you mean, in this time and place?"

"I think you know, Ailsa. You have seen a great many things happen here this evening, when the veil is thin enough to cross, and yet none of it appears to have fazed or surprised you."

"You'd be surprised by what I have seen in my life."

"I'm sure I would," he agreed, releasing her chin. "What are you doing here, Ailsa?"

She frowned, "I already told you, I heard the music and followed it."

"No. I do not mean what brought you to the glen. I am talking about what are you doing standing against this tree, instead of sitting on the cushions I left you sitting on."

She crossed her arms across her chest, put out that he was chastising her like she was a child. "I'm not a dog to sit and stay, you know," she answered, ignoring his statement regarding her not being surprised to find herself surrounded by Fae. He had his secrets, and she had her. "And Prince Orin offered to get me something to drink before I left. It seemed rude to refuse, and he was very insisting. Besides, you looked like you were busy with the blonde, so you don't have anything to lecture me about," she finished with a huff.

Abruptly grabbing her arms, Kellan pulled her away from the tree. A look of fury mixed with concern crossed his face. "Tell me you didn't drink anything he gave to you," he demanded.

Ailsa gasped at his aggressive move, "You're hurting me," she claimed, trying to yank free from his grasp.

"Look at me, Ailsa," Kellan ordered, while loosening his grip, but not removing his hold.

Blinking back the tears that sprung to her eyes, she tilted her head back and looked into his eyes. The gold shards in his blue eyes seemed to glow hot, and she felt fear for the first time in his presence. "Can you let me go, please?"

Kellan pulled her tight against his torso and wrapped his arms around her slight form. "Wish that I could. It would be so much better for the both of us if I did let you go. Something about you calls to me, Ailsa, but you are young and have yet to experience life enough to knowingly accept the things I wish of you."

Ailsa rubbed her forehead against the center of his chest. Breathing in his masculine scent, she enjoyed the feel of his arms holding her. The fear she had felt just minutes ago had been chased away, but the meaning of his words eluded her. "I don't understand?"

"I'll explain in a bit," he promised, "just tell me if you ate or drank anything Prince Orin gave you."

"Well, no," she started, "he left me here to go get something. What does it matter, anyway? You didn't have any problems sharing a drink with that blonde."

Kellan chuckled and kissed the top of her head. "What you saw, mo milis, is the lovely Devany drinking the drink I had procured for you and trying to prevent me from returning to your side. I suspect she and Orin conspired together to keep us separated. "

"Why? And why does it matter if I drink something from the hand of Prince Orin if you were getting me a drink anyway?"

"What I was going to offer you was safe for you to drink," his chest rose against her cheek as he sighed. "What I believe Orin would offer you would make it impossible for you to leave the Fae realm."

She stiffened at his words and the implication that she would have essentially been a prisoner to the Fae. Kellan stepped back and she immediately missed the warmth his body had offered. He held out his hand, "Do you trust me enough to come with me?"

Without hesitation, she placed her hand in his. At his smile, her heart skipped a beat. "Where are we going?"

"I'm going to escort you to your home. The day approaches. The veil will be thinned for another night." He gave her hand a squeeze and smiled down at her, "I suspect if your absence were detected, you would have trouble getting away to meet with me."

A spring of hope rose within her chest as his words pinged around her head, "You want to see me again?"

"I wish to get to know you better," Kellan confirmed, "and for you to get to know me better as well."

Feeling an itch at the back of her neck, Ailsa looked over her shoulder and spied Prince Orin and the blonde who had been saddling up to Kellan standing beneath the oak he had left her at. "What about Prince Orin? And why does that woman keep looking at me like she wants to skewer me?" she asked as they reached the edge of the glade.

"Prince Orin wants what was denied him, and I suppose the same could be said for Devany," he answered without looking back. "Come, day is approaching."

Together, they stepped through the thinned veil. She immediately noticed that the air didn't smell as clean and the colors seemed muted from those in the glade. Already a streak of light cut the darkness at the horizon, setting off a pulse of panic. "We have to hurry. They'll kick me out if they find me missing."

Kellan pulled her to a stop, "What do you mean, they will kick you out? Who will do this?"

"My foster parents." She pulled on his arm trying to get him moving. "If they find out I was out all night, they can kick me out of their home and I'll have to go back to the group home," she explained, happy he started moving again at her urgent pull.

"Why would your parents do such a thing?"

"They're not my parents," she answered heatedly. "They're just people the state put me with until I turn 18, and then I'm on my own."

"Where are your parents, Ailsa?" Kellan asked, his voice low and curious.

"I don't know," she responded, shrugging her shoulders, "I was found in the woods when I was 3."

"Did they not try to find you?"

"It doesn't really matter if they looked. The fact of the matter is they left me out there by myself, and were gone long enough for someone else to find me."

"Do you wish to find them...to know them and learn about your heritage?"

Something in his voice made her look up at him, but he kept his face pointing forward. "What about my heritage?"

"You have Fae blood running through your vein, mo milis. Do you not wish to know that part of who you are?"

His quick reflexes caught her before her knees hit the ground as she tripped over a tuft of grass. "How could you possibly know that?"

"I can sense it. It's one of my abilities."

"Abilities, huh? What other powers do you have?"

"I can ensure that your foster family does not detect you were absent during the night."

"That would be a pretty neat trick if you could do it, but I'm pretty sure their stupid dog will alert them to me climbing back into my window." She sighed, "We might as well slow down. If this is going to be the last time I see you, I want it to last."

Raising their clasped hands, Kellan kissed the back of her fingers, "It pleases me more than you can know that you wish to extend our time together. Have a little faith. I will do as I promise. I will keep you safe."

"Do you think I have any of these cool powers?" Ailsa asked wishfully.

Kellan came to a stop and turned towards her. With his free hand, he caressed the side of her face and tilted her chin upward. "I believe your magic has yet to show itself, but it will. Like your Fae blood, I can sense it simmering just below the surface, waiting to emerge. I have a feeling you are way more than any of us, Fae and human alike."

Looking into his eyes, Ailsa could almost believe his words. *How cool would it be to have a source of magic I could call on. Of course, I don't know a thing about wielding magic. Would I need a wand or did only witches and wizards use those like in the Harry Potter movies? One of those time turner thingies would come in handy, especially right now.*

"I can see in your eyes that you have a million questions spinning around in that fascinating mind of yours, but perhaps they can wait until this evening."

CHAPTER 4

Present Day

Touching the medallion that had hung around her neck for the last seven years, Ailsa sat on a stool behind the checkout counter of the metaphysical store she worked in. She wasn't alone. The owner, Tessa, was in the back office doing paperwork and doing what she could to keep the coffee industry in business. Still, there was no one around except the cat.

Music from the cd player filled the air and the fragrance of amber incense scented it. Together they worked to relax her while she stared out the window at the large oak sitting on the edge of the neatly manicured lawn. It welcomed the visitors as they stepped from the parking lot onto the sidewalk leading up to the door of the store. She liked to think of that old tree as the guard to the citadel. Fanciful thinking, she knew, but maybe not so far off base. After all, the store had never been robbed, which was saying something since it was located on the edge of the town limits.

The bell above the door chimed as it opened, prompting the grey long-haired cat, Arwen, to jump on the counter and voice her displeasure that her solitude had been disturbed. Ailsa scratched the feline behind her ears, earning a purr for her efforts, then a swipe of claws for daring to scratch too long.

Shaking her head, Ailsa tucked her necklace back under her collar, "Guard the cash register, Arwen," she instructed the cat, who gave her a look of disdain before curling herself up in the cushion lined box sitting next to the till. She rolled her eyes, rose from her seat, and curving her lips up into a well-practiced smile, went to greet her customer.

The combined scent of amber and sandalwood floating on the current of air that came through when the door opened niggled at her memory of Kellan. It had been seven years since she last laid eyes on him in the flesh. Seven long years. He had left his imprint on her life, and every man she tried to date didn't come close in comparison with him. *I'm doomed to spend my life waiting for a man who has probably forgotten I even exist.* She closed her eyes and inhaled, hoping to carry the smell of him with her when she fell into sleep's dark embrace later.

Two years, after the veil between the Fae and human realms fell, she started seeing Kellan in her dreams. Only there did she know the feel of his hands against her skin, the never satisfying hunger for his kiss, the taste of his sweat, and the musky scent of their bodies as they rose to the pinnacle of ecstasy and shattered together. In her dreams, she knew the feel of his arms holding her tightly against his sweat-drenched body. She'd reluctantly fall into an exhausted sleep, only to awaken to an empty room and bed, with only the phantom touch of him upon her skin.

Those nightly visits came to an abrupt stop three weeks ago. Her heart ached at the pang of loss even as her brain railed at his disappearance without out a word of goodbye. In the light of day, she knew they were just dreams. What she shared with Kellan in the recesses of her sleeping mind was not real, but it felt like it was, or had been.

The sound of a throat clearing brought Ailsa out of her out of her reverie. Looking up, her breath caught in her throat. Standing there was Kellan dressed in black leather pants that hugged his hips and muscular legs like a second skin. A white tunic tucked into his waistband with a V at the neckline offered a teasing glimpse of the chest it covered. The man who had been her dream lover and ruined any attraction to other men was now standing in front of her. Mouth open, she stood, her feet rooted to the floor, staring at him in shocked surprise, as a smirk tipped up one corner of his full lips.

"Are you not happy to see me, mo milis?" His voice was more seductive than it had been in her dreams.

Ailsa's hands curled into fists as confusion, anger, hurt, and surprise warred with one another within her. She knew what the explosive outcome would be if she didn't get a hold of her emotions. "You're about seven years late. What did you expect?"

Amusement fled his features and was replaced with remorse. "I do apologize for not returning to you the following night. Events, unforeseen, needed to be taken care of."

Ailsa crossed her arms across her chest, "You don't owe me an explanation."

"It would seem that I do," he said crossing over to her. "I can see that my attention to you in the dreaming did not erase the sting of leaving you alone when I said I would return." He raised his hand, his fingers brushing over the curve of her cheek.

Jerking her face from his touch, she frowned at him. "That...that was real?"

"Of course it was real. Did you think I would abandon you completely?"

She squinted her eyes closed. She had given him her virginity in her dreams. Did that mean she was no longer a virgin in truth? The one toy she'd been brave enough to buy and used when the need became too great to ignore would say she wasn't. "What the ever living..."

"Is there a problem, Ailsa?" The sound of Tessa's voice coming from around the corner cut off the rest of Ailsa's rant and had her eyes popping open.

"No, no problem," she replied, gritting her teeth.

Turning her attention to Kellan, Tessa's eyes widened, before she quickly bowed her head. "Prince Kellan," she stammered, "please forgive me. I was not aware it was you Ailsa was having words with."

"Your apology, though not warranted," Kellan grasped Tessa's chin between his finger and thumb, then gently lifted her face, "is accepted," he finished with a small bow of his own.

"Wait just a gosh darn minute," Ailsa spewed, "you two know each other?"

Tessa nodded while Kellan mimicked Ailsa's stance and crossed his arms across his chest, drawing her eyes to the V in tunic. Her dream memory teasing her with glimpses of her lips and tongue tracing that median line down his torso toward his impressive member, which led to other dream memories, which led to her body reacting to what were dreams but which Kellan says were real, which led to her being even more confused, which just pissed her off.

Ailsa's gaze swept from Tessa to Kellan, "Great. I'll just leave you two to catch up." Spinning on her heels, she hurriedly walked away. Furious for reasons unknown to her, she wound her way back through the store, grabbed her purse from the hook by the register, and sprinted out the door, not caring that it closed with a slam or the possibility that she may not have a job after that outburst.

*K*ellan, hearing the door shut with a bang, moved to follow Ailsa, only to be stopped by Tessa's hand on his arm. "What is your interest in my employee and friend, Kell?"

His blue and gold eyes flashed as he raised an eyebrow, "Are you questioning your Prince, Tessina?"

"Don't pull that superiority crap with me, Kellan. Just because I live mortal-side, doesn't mean I'm not still a Princess of the Fae court, or that I am not your equal."

He laughed and pulled her into an embrace. "I have missed your spunk, Sister-mine."

"Well, I haven't missed you trying to boss me around," she laughed and pushed away from him. "Seriously though, Kell. What is it you want with Ailsa? I won't have you hurt her with your games."

"You care for her?"

"I do," Tessa confirmed, sweeping her long dark hair over her shoulder. "What is she to you, Kellan?"

"I'll explain later, Tess..."

She moved to block his path. "No Kellan. You'll explain now. Ailsa is my friend and I don't have many I can call a true friend. I will not have you toying with her."

Kellan glanced down at his sister. It had been a long time since they had butted heads. He'd more than missed it, but now was not the time. He had to get to Ailsa. "What makes you think I'm playing with her?"

Tessa rolled her eyes, "You're not known for keeping company with any female for more than a night, Kellan. If all you're looking for is a tumble between the sheets, please leave Ailsa alone."

He shook his head, "I can't do that, Tessa. I have reason to believe she's in danger and right now she is running around out there with no one to protect her."

"What reason? What danger? And why do you care if she's protected or not, you just met her?"

Glaring at his sister, Kellan ran both hands through his hair and growled, "She's the gràdh mo chridhe. Until I make her mine, she's in danger."

He could feel Tessa's eyes on him as he stormed past her and out the door. Once she recovered from the shock of his declaration, she'd have questions. She always had questions, but this time he'd be more than willing to answer them. First, he had to find Ailsa.

CHAPTER 5

*B*eneath the drooping branches of a willow tree, Ailsa sat with her back against its trunk, staring at the pond. It's mirrored surface disturbed by the current of a lone duck paddling its way from one shoreline to the other. Wrapping her arms around her bent legs, she rested her cheek on top of her knees.

"Really, running away to hide? You're a frickin' coward, Ailsa," she ridiculed herself. Sighing, she sat up, slipped her feet from their ballet flats, and folded her legs into a pretzel under the wide expanse of her skirt. Her arms rose above her head, palm meeting palm. Eyes closed, she took a deep breath, letting it out as her elbows bent and palms still connected, her arms stretched out in front of her. A sense of calm and clear headedness coursed through her as she repeated the breathing exercise four more times, before the pendant warmed against her chest.

"Are you done hiding, mo milis?"

Ailsa froze and opened her eyes to find Kellan crouched down in front of her. "How did you find me?"

Amusement teased the corners of his lips. Something softer, almost endearing shone from his eyes. The face she knew so well in her dreams and memories of their short time together in the glade tempted her to reach out and trace its contours with her fingers. Lowering her arms, she tucked her hands beneath her thighs in the feeble hope she could fight the temptation he represented. At least until she got some answers.

"May I join you?"

Her knee jerk reaction was to deny his request, but saying no wouldn't get her the answers she wanted. If she were being truthful with herself, she didn't want him to leave. She wanted what they had shared in the dreaming. She needed it like she needed her next breath. She wanted something to remember and carry with her when he left again. So she would gather as many moments with him as she could. When she was once more alone, she'd pull out each treasured memory, bask in what once was, and then safely tuck them back in the vault of her heart, guarding them as diligently as a dragon watching over its gold. She was alone in this world, she had long came to terms with that fact, but she could have this.

"Ailsa?" Kellan's voice pulled her from her inner musings.

"What?"

"May I join you?" he asked again.

Grabbing the moments, she reminded herself, before nodding, "Of course." She cringed at the breathy tone of her voice. If Kellan noticed, he didn't react. She wasn't sure if she was relieved he hadn't heard her, or if she was pissed that he had and chose to ignore it. She was a walking, talking contradiction where he was concerned. Surprising her even more, instead of sitting beside her, he plopped his leather clad behind right in front of her, mimicking the lotus position she was in. She held her breath as one of his knees made contact with one of hers. Even through the leather, she could feel the heat of his body, from that one contact point, spread through her body, making it yearn for more.

"Why did you run, Ailsa? Were you not pleased to see me?"

She pressed her thighs down, making sure her hands were

securely trapped beneath them, suppressing the urge to trace her fingertips along the outline of his lips. "Should I have been pleased to see you?" she asked, cocking her head to the side.

"Well I'm certainly glad to see you."

"Good for you. What are you doing here?"

Kellan's grin looked as if he could see through her nonchalance, "I did promise you I would be back for you."

"Seven years ago. You left it a bit late don't you think?" she huffed, "Besides, what makes you think I've been sitting around waiting for you?"

A high-pitched squeal filled the air. Ailsa realized it came from her when she unexpectedly found herself flipped around and sitting in the shallow bowl created by Kellan's folded legs, the hem of her skirt rising up to settle just above her knees.

"You are mine, Ailsa. No other shall ever have you."

Her back against his chest, his chin rested on top of her head as his arms wrapped around her torso. He effectively had her trapped, his body and limbs a prison she wasn't sure she wanted to be free of but she'd be damned if she would let him think he had conquered her. "Let. Me. Go," she demanded through grit teeth, pinching at his leg with her now free fingers.

"I know you don't really want me to do that." Kellan responded, the timbre of his voice sending shivers down her spine.

She squeezed her eyes and thighs close, fighting the spark of desire he lit in her. "You don't know me at all."

He lowered his head until his lips brushed the tip of her ear, "Oh but I do. I know every inch of you. His teeth scraped her earlobe as his mouth continued its downward travel journey bringing his lips to the curve of her neck. "I know that biting you right here," he bit down, capturing the tender flesh between his teeth, then let go, licking the sting away with the flat of his tongue, "gets you wet."

A cry escaped her lips as the painful pinch morphed into

something pleasurable. She tilted her neck to the side giving him more access and silently asking for more.

Kellan's hands, finding their way beneath her sweater, slid up her torso. "Are you wet for me, mo milis?" he asked, pulling the cups of her bra down, freeing her breasts.

She arched her back, pushing the throbbing tips of her nipples into his palms, needing more than the soft caresses he was giving them. "Kellan," she pleaded, her legs scissoring against each other trying to ease the ache building at her core. She gripped his thighs, her head moving restlessly against his shoulder as his warm, wet mouth continued its sensual assault against the side of her neck.

"Tell me what I want to hear and I'll give you what you need." he prodded, flicking her nipple with the tip of his fingers of one hand. His other hand slid down her torso to find its way beneath the waistband of her skirt, "Are you wet for me, Ailsa? Shall I find out for myself?" he asked, his fingers teasing the skin above the top of her panties.

"Yes..." she gasped. Her body writhed with need. The hard length of his cock pressed against her back, bringing to mind the dream memory of what it was like to have him fill her, stretch her inner walls, and consume her completely.

"What do we have here?" he asked, slipping his hand in to her panties. He slid a finger between the cleft of her swollen lips, before withdrawing his hand. She whimpered at the loss of his touch. "Look at that," he whispered in her ear, "you're soaked."

Ailsa flushed in embarrassment at the sight of his fingers, damp with her juices. Before she could push away from his hard body, she found herself lying on her back atop the soft moss that covered the ground, with her skirt raised above her waist and Kellan kneeling between her trembling legs.

"I need to taste you, Ailsa," Kellan's voice husky with desire sent shivers down up her spine, and she could feel herself getting wetter as his eyes travelled down her exposed body with unbanked lust shimmering in his eyes. "If you don't want this," her hips rose to meet the stroke of his fingers along the seam where her legs and pelvis met, "you need only say no." His thumbs caressed the sensitive skin of her inner thighs, "Yay or nay, mo milis?"

"Yes." Her whispered reply was followed by the sound of Kellan ripping her drenched panties off her body.

"Take off your sweater and bra, Ailsa," he demanded. "Let me see those beautiful breasts."

Her hands shaking, she sat up enough to do as he asked. Lying back down, a shiver coursed through her. She wasn't sure if it was because of the cool breeze brushing against her exposed skin, or if it was the feeling of being prey about to be pounced on by a predator with nothing on his mind but to devour her.

"You're perfection," Kellan declared rising over her. His mouth and fingers played her body as if it were a fiddle and he was a master tuner, plucking nerve endings that resonated all the way down to her core, and her cries mingled with his grunts were the accompanying orchestra.

His lips travelled down the center of her torso, stopping at the top of her mound. "You're mine," he declared, bending down between her damp thighs. Her legs held wide by his broad shoulders, his fingers spread her nether lips. With the tip of his nose pressing against her clit, he inhaled. A primal growl filled the air as he swiped his tongue down her middle, lapping up her nectar before he speared the tip of it inside her, igniting her already sensitive nerve endings.

"Kellan, please..." she pleaded, grabbing his hair. She vacillated between pushing him away to make the cresting tide building within her stop before it drowned her and never wanting the pleasure to end.

Masterfully, his tongue moved to tease her pulsing nub as a finger played at the opening of her core. Flicking his tongue and nibbling on her growing clit, Ailsa wriggled under him wanting more. His mouth devoured her. Crooked fingers strummed a bundle of nerves building her excitement. Resting her pointed toes on the tops of his shoulders, she arched her back, pressing her sex against his beautiful mouth, taking every stroke he gave. Her hips rocked in time with his seeking fingers. With one last thrust, her body shattered in ecstasy as she fisted her hands in his hair and shrieked his name.

CHAPTER 6

Kellan's eyes opened to the sound of wind rustling the leaves of the willow tree and the slight weight of Ailsa draped across his chest, one of her legs nestled between his. His arms were full with one hand on her arm while the other rested on the small of her back. For once, in the seven mortal years they had been separated, the clawing fear that she would be taken from him before he could claim her loosened its grip on his heart.

Tilting his head to the side, he gazed down at her sleeping face and smiled. He had his mate safe in his arms. He had no doubt he was in for a tongue lashing when she woke up, now that the cloud of lust had abated, but he was looking forward to it and to a tongue lashing of different type when the last of her anger was extinguished. Pressing his lips to the top of Ailsa's dark head, his hand slid over the lush mound of her ass.

A groan rumbled in his chest as she stirred in her sleep. Her knee brushed against his balls, awakening his slumbering cock, which was quick to remind him that it hadn't found its release in the tight, wet channel that was his to plunder, though he had almost spilled himself into his pants. Watching her shatter, with the sweet and tangy flavor of her juices on his tongue and lips, and hearing her call out his name in her fevered ecstasy as her inner walls clamped down on his fingers about did him in. It took all his control and then some to not undo his pants right then and there and take her.

Ever so slowly, his fingers cinched up Ailsa's skirt. The cool breath of the wind brushed over his seeking hand and the pale flesh of her exposed behind. The cawing of a raven not far away brought his mind back to the reason, or one of the reasons he had shown up unexpectedly. Reluctantly, he covered Ailsa's bare skin, willing his erection to stand down.

Wrapping his arms around her slight form, he pressed his lips to the top of her head. "Ailsa..." he whispered, "it's time to wake up." He smiled at the sound of her small whimper as she buried his face into his chest.

Between one breath and the next, her body stiffened against his and he knew awareness had come floating back to Ailsa. It was a good thing he had thought to seal them in what amounted to a privacy bubble before he had crawled beneath the drooping branches to join her. It let the sounds of the world come through, but noises from within the bubble dissipated once they made contact with the invisible wall.

Raising her hands between their bodies, Ailsa pushed against his chest. After holding on to her a little longer, he loosened his hold on her, watching as she sat up and scurried backwards to her discarded sweater and bra. His eyes watched her hands shakily don her clothing, hiding the ivory expanse of pale skin still flushed with sleep, from his admiring eyes. He bit back a smile at the sight of her green eyes burning bright with the heat of her anger. Or was it embarrassment?

"How dare you..."

"I would dare much, Ailsa," he nipped her tirade in the bud, "and I didn't hear you complain as you came beautifully on my tongue and fingers." He pinned her with a pointed stare, daring her to deny the veracity of his words, "But tell me, why exactly are you angry with me at this very moment." He thought he knew, but he wanted, needed, to hear it from her own lips. He needed to know how much atonement he needed to make for his absence.

"What are you doing here, Kellan?" The scent of hurt coloring her words belied the cool tone she tried to affect. "Did you all of a sudden get an itch to try out the pitiful human you met so long ago?"

Fury that she would talk about herself as if she were anything other than perfect boiled up in him. "You will not talk about yourself in such a way, Ailsa. Do you understand me?"

Tilting up her stubborn chin, Ailsa crossed her arms, and glared at him, "I'll talk about myself any way I want to, and there's not a damn thing you can do about it. You have absolutely no say whatsoever about what goes on in my life."

"That's where you are wrong, mo milis," he countered. "You pledged yourself to me seven years ago and agreed to wear the pendant now resting between your beautiful breasts." Her hand reaching for and wrapping around the pendant elicited a smile from his lips. "You re-established that pledge when you gave yourself completely to me in the dreaming."

A frown creased her brow as confusion clouded her eyes, "I did not give myself to you in the dreaming."

"Indeed you did."

She shook her head, "That can't have been real. It was only a dream."

"Just because it was but a dream, doesn't mean it wasn't real, Ailsa. I explained this before you gifted me with your maidenhood."

Her shoulders rounded, "So what, did you just come here to make sure that I spend the rest of my life alone?"

Standing, Kellan crossed the short distance between them and knelt before her huddled form, "What makes you think you will be spending the rest of your life alone?" he asked, raising his hand to stroke her cheek.

She leaned her face into his palm before jerking back and looking away, "You just admitted to marking me in such a way that no other man would try to approach me. I'm not a tree to be sprayed like a dog marking its territory."

Kellan reached out, grabbing a handful of her dark, silky tresses close to her scalp. His grip firm, her turned her face back toward him, then pulled downward so she had no other choice but to look up at him. Her lips parted in surprise. Resisting the urge no longer, he closed his over hers.

His tongue swept over hers. She was stiff before giving in and sinking into the kiss with ferocity to match his own. His free arm wrapped around her back and lifted her to straddle his thighs. A moan reverberated in his chest as she wrapped her legs around his hips, her arms around his shoulders, then rocked her sex against his aroused shaft, surrounding it with her feminine heat. He tore his mouth away, "You are not a tree or any other inanimate object that a dog would need to mark. You are my mate. There is nothing in the universe that will tear you from my side. You are mine, Ailsa, in as much as I am yours."

Face flushed, Ailsa's breath came in shallow pants, "So you say," the tip of her pink tongue darted out across her kiss swollen lips. "Now prove it," she challenged him before crawling off his lap. He watched her straighten her clothing and smooth a hand down her hair. Flashing him a dare with her eyes, she turned her back and walked through the branches of the willow. Luckily, his mind wasn't so befuddled with lust that he forgot to dissolve the privacy barrier allowing her to pass unhindered.

Rising to his feet, he brushed off the debris on his clothing, then followed his mate out into the world. He had the feeling she was going to lead him on a merry chase, but in the end, he would have his prize.

CHAPTER 7

Turning off the now cold water, Ailsa wrapped the large terrycloth towel around her torso, slid the plexi-glass door open, and stepped out of the tub onto the plush, purple rug. Her damp feet padded across the cold black and white octagonal tile floor to the vanity. She smiled as the bathroom door opened wide enough to allow Midnight, the black cat who'd adopted her, to enter. There was no doubt in her mind that he had sat outside the door until he was sure her shower was complete and the water was turned off. He'd learned his lesson after walking along the edge of the tub, only to slip and fall into the spraying water. He'd given her a look of disgust which had set loose the peal of laughter she'd been holding in. He'd jumped back out of tub, shook the water off his fur, and yowled at her as he strolled out the door, the tip of his ramrod tail, high in the air, gave a flick, and she'd wondered if that was his way of flipping her off.

Holding the towel at her chest, she bent down to scratch Midnight behind his silky ear as he butted her calf with his head before weaving his way between her ankles. "Are you staying out of trouble?" she asked as she stood back up. He chirruped his reply followed by series of purrs before jumping onto the toilet seat and curling into a ball to wait for her to finish her routine.

Skin moisturized and tangles brushed from her still damp hair, she pulled the door open. "Are you coming or staying?" she asked the napping feline. He raised the lid of one green eye, only to close it again, as if to say, *'Go away, I'm napping.'* Shaking her head, Ailsa rolled her eyes. "Suit yourself," she responded, flicking the light switch off.

Padding down the hallway, she chuckled as Midnight darted past her toward the living area of her small apartment. Her mind replaying the encounter with Kellan beneath the willow tree, she blindly made her way over the carpet of the living space to the vinyl flooring of the kitchenette. She stopped in front of the refrigerator. Hand gripping the handle, she bent her head down with her eyes squeezed shut. Why had she run from him? What happened to grabbing each moment with the greed of a child in a candy store?

Her head shot up and a scream erupted from her throat as two large hands gripped her hips from behind. Terror flooding her body, she clawed at the hands holding her and kicked her heels trying to cause what damage she could.

"Be still, mo milis," Kellan's husky voice coaxed. He wrapped his arms around hers, pulling her flush against his hard body.

Fear, relief, and anger flooded through her. Her heart was beating so hard and fast Ailsa wondered if it would explode out her chest. She took a deep breath and willed her body to go still. *Talk about being between a rock and a hard place,* the random assessment flitted through her scrambled thoughts of how to escape. Her head bent forward and shot back striking his sternum. At the loosening of his grip, she dropped to the floor between his legs and the refrigerator. The sound of Kellan's "oof" gave a small measure of satisfaction, though she had no doubt that it was surprise, not pain, which had elicited the reaction from him. Scurrying across the floor, she gained her feet on the other side of the counter separating the kitchen from the living room.

"Not to sound repetitious, but what are you doing here, Kellan? How did you find me?" she asked, tightening the towel that was threatening to come loose.

"You look quite fetching in that towel, gràdh mo chridhe," he responded with a licentious grin on his face. "However," he continued, moving toward her, "I believe you're lovelier without it."

Crossing her legs, she squeezed her thighs against each other, trying to stem the throb of desire. "Sooo not an answer to either of my questions, Kellan."

"It wasn't, but it doesn't negate the validity of my observation."

She scowled, he grinned and kept coming in her direction. "Stop," she ordered raising her arm. A ball of energy pulsed brightly against her outstretched palm. With a thought, it flew from her hand, hitting Kellan in the center of his chest.

Smiling broadly, his body seemingly absorbing the energy ball she just threw at him Kellan kept moving forward. Every step brought him closer to her. "A spell is only as good as the intent, Ailsa. You say you want me to stop, but that's not what you really want. Is it?" He reached up and wrapped his hand around her outstretched wrist.

"I want you to stop whatever game you're playing," she responded as he pulled on her wrist, forcing her upper body to lean over the countertop. "Let go," she demanded, her free hand holding the towel in place.

"Never." His blue eyes darkened, "I will never let you go, Ailsa."

She yanked on her arm free from his grip. There was no doubt that she only managed that feat because he chose to let go. "You didn't want me before. What's changed?"

He stared at her with an incredulous look on his face. "Not want you? I have wanted you since I first laid eyes on you."

Standing upright, Ailsa squelched the tingle of pleasure his words invoked. "You could have fooled me," she retorted, pushing away from the counter and walking to the window in the living room.

"There were reasons for my absence."

"Reasons that are for only for you to know, I'm sure."

She shuddered as his hands gently clapped onto her shoulders and slid down her arms. She hadn't even heard him move. "They are my own and I will tell you of them. But for now, go get dressed." Kissing the top of her head, he turned her in the direction of the hall. "You in naught but that towel is too tempting a distraction," he confessed, giving her a gentle push to move.

Ailsa, stopping at the entrance of the hall, looked over her shoulder. "It's good to see you again, Kellan," she softly stated. Face flushed with embarrassment over the admission she never thought she'd make, Ailsa fled down the hall without waiting to hear his response.

CHAPTER 8

*K*ellan paced the floor of the sitting area, which consisted of a small tan settee, a chair by the window, and a short wall lined with three bookcases. This apartment was little better than the home he'd left her at all those years ago. Seven mortal years. He had not taken into account the time difference between realms when he had left her with the promise to return. On one hand, it ate at his gut that he had left her alone for so long. On the other, she had probably been safer tucked away in the human world than in Faerie when the walls fell and chaos reigned supreme. His steps led him to the window. Peering out over the landscape, his memories took him to when he had returned her to the house she lived in with the parents who were not her parents.

*S*even Years Ago

She's lovely, Kellan thought. A pale flush stained her cheeks, her green eyes sparkled with wonder and excitement at all she had seen. She tilted her face up. The tip of her tongue darting out to moisten her lips challenged his self-control to not claim her mouth and taste her. He knew she was waiting for a kiss. He did the only thing he could do. He'd cupped her cheeks in between his palms and pressed his lips to her forehead, then stepped back.

He suppressed a smile at her frown and pout. "Lead the way to your room, pet, before you make me forget myself." Never had he concerned himself with taking or doing what he wanted and the consequences be damned. She was different. He planned on keeping her, but he had to give her time to mature and know her own mind and heart. The court would eat up and spit out an innocent such as she, if she didn't know how to hold her own.

"You can leave me here," Ailsa had proclaimed, her eyes darting away from his.

"I'll see you safely inside, Ailsa."

"But..."

"No buts. If you are in such a hurry to be rid of my company, you best get moving."

Without another word, she turned and walked toward the back of the house. For a moment he wondered if she was really in a rush to be rid of him, but her posture dispelled that errant thought. She'd folded her arms across her midsection, her shoulders were rounded over, and her head was bowed. Where was the spirited sprite who had stood toe to toe with him? Who was this dejected creature before him now? Rounding the back corner of the house, he was surprised when she continued, walking past the door, coming to a stop before a small open window.

"You can go now."

"This is hardly seeing you inside, Ailsa. I am curious, however," he continued despite the dismissive shrug of her shoulders, "why are we standing beneath a window instead of going through the door?"

Surprised horror flashed across her features, "You don't really mean to go inside do you?"

"That's what 'I'll see you safely inside' would imply don't you think?"

"No...no," she shook her head, "I thought you were just going to make sure I got home safely. Not that you were actually going to come into the house." She closed the gap between them, placing her hand on his chest. "They don't know I left. If they catch you inside, they'll throw me out for sure."

He gathered her in his arms. Holding her close, he sent soothing waves of calm to her, chasing away the tide of panic he had felt building within her. The songs of nature stirring to greet the day reached his ears, warning him of the approaching dawn. With a thought, he sifted them back through time and space into her sparsely furnished room right next to the bed. The moon sat high on her perch in the night sky and the only song floating in the air was that of those creatures who claimed the night as their own. She needn't know that the few hours she had spent in Faerie, when she crossed the veil, had actually been days in the human realm, or the fear she had of being found missing had been realized. He'd only taken them back to the time right after she entered the glen, but it was enough so as to not alter her present. Reluctantly, he let her go and took a step back.

Ailsa's head swiveled from side to side. "How did you do that?"

Kellan smiled broadly at the look of amazement on her face. "Just a touch of Fae magick."

Her hand rising up to cover a yawn, she nodded, "Cool."

"I have a gift for you." Around her neck, he draped a pendant made of Athair-Luss, ground ivy, hanging from a silver chain. Etched into the round disk was a circle intersected by two crossing lines sitting beneath an arch. It would not only offer her protection, it would keep her hidden from the Fae who had seen her in the glen. Lifting her hair, he freed the chain from her dark tresses, enjoying the feel of the silky strands sliding over his fingers.

Her hand immediately closed around the wooden disc. "No

one's ever given me a gift," she replied. She looked up at him, her green eyes swimming in pools of unshed tears, "I...I can't accept it."

He clasped her hands in his, stalling her motion to unclasp the chain, "Of course you can."

"They'll think I've stolen it."

"Do you want to keep it, Ailsa?" he asked, touching his forehead to hers.

"Yes. But..."

"There are no 'buts'. It is yours. A gift from a prince to one he favors." Tilting her chin up, he gently swiped away the tears staining her cheeks. "It would be rude to refuse to accept that which was freely given," he added, knowing how she felt about being rude. It was a dirty trick of manipulation, but if it would keep her safe, he was all for it. She looked incredibly beguiling, standing before him, the edge of her top teeth running over her bottom lip.

"Why would you give me this?" she asked, bewildered.

He debated on whether or not to tell her the complete truth or not. He couldn't outright lie to her. He didn't want to either, but he also had no wish to scare her. However, perhaps if she knew the whole of it, she would take care. So young and oblivious, she was clueless to the petty jealousies that ran through the court. The Fae were not used to rejection, and there were two who'd been soundly rejected this very night. They would not take it well.

Kellan traced the tip of a finger down the side of her neck to the base of her throat where the pendant rested. "I give this to you for two reasons. One, I wish for you to have something of me to hold onto until I can return."

He smiled as she swayed on tired legs. Reaching down, he grabbed the edge of the blankets on the bed and pulled them back. "In you go."

Looking at him, then the bed, and back to him again, one slow blink followed another. "What?" she asked perplexed.

"Get in the bed, Ailsa, before you fall on your face from

exhaustion," he explained while placing his hand on her lower back and giving her a nudge to move.

"But what was the second reason?" she climbed in, settling her head on the flat pillow, and resting her arms on top of the blankets he'd pulled up to her chest.

Sitting on the edge of the mattress, Kellan clasped one of her hands in his, "The second," he started, running his thumb over the soft skin on the back of her hand, "is for your protection. Prince Orin was deprived of his prey, and the fact that I chose you over the lovely Devany will not sit well with her fragile ego. This pendant will protect you from those who would do you harm, and hide you from the Fae who might seek retribution."

Ailsa shook her head, "But, I'm nobody. I'm nothing compared to them."

"You are everything," he refuted. "Promise me you will not take it off, Ailsa."

"I don't think they see me as a threat, but if it'll make you feel better, I promise to wear it."

The tight band around his lungs loosened at her promise, and he breathed deeply for the first time since placing the necklace around her slender neck. With a sigh, he bent down, his cheek resting against hers, "Sleep, mo milis." Sitting up, he watched her eyelids lose the battle to stay open. She took in a deep breath, her body relaxing as the whisper of her exhale brushed across the back of his hand. "Stay out of the glen, Ailsa. It isn't safe for you there."

Sure she was well on her way to the dream realm, Kellan rose from his seat. Reaching down, he lifted a thick strand of her dark hair that had fallen across her face when she turned onto her side, and tucked it over her shoulder.

His eyes landed on a crescent moon shape just behind her ear where the base of her skull met the column of her neck. Unbidden, the tip of his finger traced over the mark he knew so well because it matched the one he had. It wasn't as dark as it would get once they intimately joined their bodies. He knew he wanted to keep her, but this was proof that the Goddess had indeed chosen a true mate for him and had possibly been the guiding force that brought them together. And now, he had to leave her, but first he would make sure these foster parents of her treated her like the princess she was.

∾

*P*resent Day

*A*ilsa threw on a pair of leggings, the oversized sweatshirt she'd found at the thrift shop, and a pair of thick slouchy socks. Taking a deep breath, she pulled back her shoulder, and opened the door. For a brief second she wondered if Kellan had left. Her heart sank a little at the thought, but the feel of his energy permeating the hall banished that depressing thought. Shaking her head, she admitted to herself that she was being a flip-flopper of the highest degree. She wanted him to leave then she wanted him to stay. She wanted him to explain his absence but then she didn't care about anything other than his being there. She wanted him to find her sexy and desirable, but then she dressed like she was going to spend the day sitting on her couch watching DVD's on television.

She reached the end of the hall in time to see Kellan reaching down to grab Midnight by the scruff of his neck and pull him off his leg. He raised him to eye level where they seemed to be having a staring contest. His tail swishing side to side, Midnight slowly blinked his eyes as if he had zero damns to give and could do this all day. And really, he was a cat, so he probably could. Ailsa's hand covered her mouth, stifling a laugh as Kellan's voice ended the silent standoff. "Are we going to have a problem?" he challenged the feline. A swipe of his claws, which narrowly missed Kellan's chin, was Midnight's only response before twisting his body, escaping the prince's clutches, and then darting past Ailsa down the hall.

Returning her attention back to the male standing in her living room who'd turned and was now facing her. "Are you butting heads with my cat?" she asked, resisting the urge to fan her face, as his eyes roamed over her body with a heated caress.

"Just a difference of opinion," he smirked.

"Really?" She arched a brow as her feet, seeming to have a mind of their own, crossed the floor to where he stood in front of her window. "About what?"

Kellan shrugged his shoulders, "He was under the impression that my leg was a pin cushion for his claws. I made sure he knew the error of his thinking."

She stopped in front of him, less than six inches stretched between the tips of their toes and yet it could have been miles. Looking up at him, her fingers itched to thread their way into his dark hair. She licked her lips. His eyes flared with unbaked desire. "Why are you really here, Kellan?"

His hand reached up, tucked a lock of hair behind her ear, causing her to shiver when his fingers brushed against the sensitive crescent shaped birthmark hidden beneath her hair. He gave her a knowing smile as if he knew what his touch in that particular spot did to her. "Is it so hard to believe I came back for you?"

"But why?"

Kellan took her hand, "Let's sit while we discuss this, shall we?"

Ailsa looked down so he wouldn't see her eye roll, but let him lead her to the floral loveseat where they sat in opposite corners facing each other. Like with whatever room he occupied, Kellan sitting on her loveseat made it seem smaller than when she sat on it by herself. Picking up a throw pillow, she held it against her torso. "Okay. I'm ready to hear what you have to tell me."

"I don't want you to just hear me, Ailsa," he responded,

scooting even closer to her. "I want you to listen to what I'm saying. Not with your head," he continued, tracing his thumb across her brow then placed his palm against her chest, "but with your heart. Can you do that, mo milis?"

Gone was the charming flirt. Beneath his intense stare, her heart pounded against her chest. "Yes," she whispered, nodding. Once her answer slipped past her lips, an epiphany that her life was about to change washed over her.

CHAPTER 9

Walking up the stairs to her apartment, the tip of Ailsa's finger traced over the crescent mark beneath her hairline. What she had always thought was a birthmark, turned out to be a sign the Goddess marked her as a true mate, and Kellan had a matching mark in the same spot. She was his and he was hers. Her mind was reeling. She wasn't even a full-blood Fae. How any of this was possible, she didn't know. She was fighting hard to keep that open mind she'd promised Kellan.

Ailsa opened her door, nearly falling on her behind as her foot slid out from under her when she stepped on a grey envelope that appeared to have been slipped under the door. Picking up the offending stationary, her ears picked up the sound of the shower running. Peeling off her coat, she set it along with her purse on the couch.

"Is that Kellan in the shower?" she asked Midnight as he twined his way between her ankles. He mewed, abandoning his circuit and made his way to the kitchen, sure she would follow. Reaching into the cabinet, Ailsa grabbed a can of cat food. Midnight jumped onto the counter and batted at her hand holding the bowl with his meal. "You know you're not supposed to be up there," she admonished the cat, setting the bowl in front of him. He sat staring at her, dismissal in his feline eyes. "You could show a little gratitude, you know," she responded to his silent command that she let him eat in peace. Shaking her head, Ailsa left him to his meal and made her way to her bedroom room to discard her clothing before continuing to the bathroom and the man who stood in her shower. Her mate. Hers. Her heart skipped with joy at the thought that the universe had gifted her with a mate that was always intended for her.

She closed the door behind her, letting her eyes drink in the masculine beauty of Kellan. Water sluiced down the contours of his body, like a lovers kiss traveling down the planes of muscle. Her gaze stopped at the sight of his hand surrounding his erect cock, slowly sliding up and down.

"See something you like, gràdh mo chridhe?" he asked, drawing her attention to his face.

"I was going to offer to wash your back, but I see you have everything well in hand," she retorted with a smirk.

He slid the glass door open and extended his hand out to her. "My back is good, but I have other body parts that might appreciate your attention."

She crossed the short distance between the door and the shower, shedding her clothing, all the while aware of his eyes following the sway of her hips. The knowledge that he wanted her as much as she wanted him made her confidence soar with every step. Placing her hand in his, she stepped over the side of the tub into his arms. Hands braced on his upper arms, her breasts pushed against his chest and the hard length of his shaft pressed against her abdomen. Gazing up into his beautiful face, Ailsa's mind reeled with the thought of how 'real' the moment felt. Kellan's touch, in her dreams, were a lost memory compared to the electricity that was streaming through every pore of her body.

Kellan's hand fisting the hair at the back of her head brought her to her senses just as his lips crashed down on hers. Her hands gripped him tighter as their kiss intensified. The silkiness of his tongue slid over her lips, her mouth, begging her to let him have it all. The cool water ran in streams down Ailsa's scorching body, her mind soaking in every touch, every caress. Breaking the kiss and tugging her hair, Kellan trailed soft kisses down her neck, fire exploding each time his tongue flicked against her skin. His hands maneuvered down her wet back, turning her body just as his engorged cock nudged her against the shower wall.

A soft moan escaped her lips as Kellan's hot mouth closed over her hard nipple and his hands clenched her ass. Ailsa could barely breathe. Her core throbbed with every suck, every nibble, every tug that he gave her slick breast.

Panting in the sheer delight of their ecstasy, she stood on tiptoe and slid her leg up his thigh wanting more. As if taking his cue, Kellan lifted her ever so slightly positioning himself under her, heat radiating from her source of pleasure. In one quick thrust, he melded himself with her, both of them gasping from the magnitude of their frenzy. Holding her tight, he pumped his sheath in her wet folds, the intoxication of their love-making sweeping over them both.

Ailsa buried her head in his neck riding him as he moaned in pleasure. Each thrust bringing them closer to release. Water flowed over their body, her nails dug into his back as her womanhood tightened around his magnificent cock. Panting and moaning, their bodies strained for release.

"Now, mo milis, now!" With one last deep stroke, their bodies erupted in sheer rapture. A thousand lights shone bright as she closed her eyes never wanting that moment to end. Hanging on to one another as the last quiver of release overtook their senses, Ailsa knew that they were truly meant for each...mind, body, and soul.

CHAPTER 10

Slipping into her favorite blue maxi dress, Ailsa padded barefoot from her room to the kitchen, loving the twinge lingering in her thighs, a delicious indicator of all the ways Kellan had taken her over the last two days. In between talking, they had christened every surface in her small apartment. Even the walls hadn't escaped their amorous activities. Always a fast healer, thanks to her Fae blood, Ailsa knew the ache would soon be gone, but for now, she loved the reminder, as if she could forget.

A glass of water in hand, her eyes landed on the grey envelope sticking out from under the refrigerator. Taking a sip, she set the glass down, and walked over to retrieve the envelope. A frown creased her brow. On the front was her name in an elaborate script. There wasn't a return address. Curious, Ailsa turned it over. A tingle started in her hands and slid up her arms as her fingernail freed flap open and pulled out the stationary inside. Opening the card, she coughed as a waft of sweet smelling powder floated from its confines into her lungs. Eyes watering, she took a deep breath and read the message within.

> *Now is the time*
> *What's yours is mine*
> *Return to the glen*
> *The start and the end*
> *Hand and heart*
> *Heart and hand*
> *A lover's kiss to forget*

The words flared with light, catching her off guard. She shook her head against the onslaught of vertigo assailing her as she watched the card slip from her fingers and float to the floor.

"Ailsa."

The sound of Kellan's voice booming down the hall brought her out of the haze. She walked over to the mouth of the hall, drinking in the sight of him standing at the entrance of the bathroom, the light behind him casting him in a golden glow. "You bellowed?"

Coming toward her, Kellan chuckled. "I was hoping you'd join me in the shower."

Shaking her head, she smiled at the hint of a sulk in his voice. "Uh-uh." *He doesn't walk,* she thought, *he stalks. A predator with his eyes on his prey. Confidence in each languid step that he would come out on top.* Funny enough, Ailsa was more than okay with that, but it didn't stop her from taking a step back. "You promised me chocolate croissants after your talk with Tessa."

His hands reached out, grabbing hold of her hips, and pulling her toward him. Pelvis to pelvis, his arousal, making itself known against her belly, re-ignited the flames of her own desires. She stared up at his face, getting lost in fathomless depths of his brilliant blue eyes.

"I can think of something I'd rather do than talk with my sister," he countered, his husky voice seducing her senses.

Sliding her hands up his chest and over his shoulders, her breath escaped her parted lips in silent invitation. He lowered his face to hers, his intent more than clear and wanted. His lips a breath away from her, her stomach growled letting its objection to this unplanned seduction be known.

While her face flushed with embarrassment, Kellan's roar of laughter filled the air. Pressing a kiss to her forehead, he took a step back. "You make me forget all about my chivalrous intentions," he proclaimed, reaching down to adjust the bulge pressing against the front of his pants.

Taking her hand in his, he pulled her to the door. "Are you sure you don't want to go with me?"

Ailsa shook her head, "No. Tessa deserves to have some of your undivided attention. I still can't believe she's your sister."

"Promise me you won't leave the apartment. I've set wards to keep any unwanted visitors out, but the hiding spell on your amulet became ineffective when you reached the Fae equivalent of maturity and discovered your own powers. We'll work on strengthening them and exploring all you are capable of doing soon, but I'd feel better if you weren't out in the open without me."

Ailsa could see the genuine concern etched across his face and shimmering in his blue eyes that only minutes ago were simmering with unadulterated lust, and nodded. She didn't think anyone would come for her, but she could do this for him. "I promise. I'll stay here and wait for you." Pressing her body against his, she placed her hands at the back of his neck, "If you hurry, maybe we can see how different the chocolate tastes when we lick it off parts of our bodies."

Standing on her toes, she ran the tip of her tongue up the column of his neck and along his jaw line. She smiled as his hands gripped her ass, pulling her tight against him as he thrust his cock against her belly. The low growl reverberating in his chest seemed to have a direct link to her core, make it pulse with need and become wet with anticipation of his possession. Another rolling rumble from her stomach had them both smiling and shaking their heads.

He kissed the tip of her nose. "I see I'm going to have to feed one hunger before I can satisfy on another."

"I'll make it worth your wait," she promised, giving him what she hoped was a sultry smile.

"I'm sure you will," he responded, tilting her chin up with the side of his finger.

His mouth closed over hers, stealing her breath with the intensity of his bone-melting kiss and the promise of more to come. All too soon for her liking, he broke the kiss and stepped back, holding on to her arms until he was sure she was steady on her feet.

Opening the door, he gave her a smug smirk, "I'll be back soon."

"Promise?" she asked, breathlessly?

"I swear with all that I am, I will always return to you," he vowed.

Ailsa nodded and smiled. A sense of foreboding flooded her as he closed the door behind him. A wave of dizziness crashed into her head. Stumbling back against the wall, she slowly lowered herself to the floor then slipped into darkness.

Ailsa frowned as a furry paw batted impatiently at her chin. Awareness came rushing back at the ache of hips against a hard surface and the realization she wasn't lying on the comfortable softness of her mattress. Had she fallen off her bed in her sleep? Forcing her eyelids open, she looked around her living room in confusion. How did she end up taking a snooze by her apartment door?

She squeezed her eyes shut, trying to recall what lead up to her sitting on the floor. All she could remember was sitting on the stool in Tessa's metaphysical store. A thick haze blanketed everything after that moment. A stab of pain pulsed at her temple as she tried mentally pushing the fog away, leaving her gasping for air.

Her breath coming out in shallow pants, Ailsa scrambled to her feet, upending Midnight who'd been sitting on her lap.

Pressing a hand to her heaving chest, she couldn't seem to take in enough air. Her gaze landed on her coat lying across the back of the couch and the keys sitting on top. *I'm late. I have to go,* she thought, immediately popping the bubble of panic she'd felt rising in her chest.

Snatching up her keys, she rushed to leave, almost tripping over Midnight who darted across her path. "Midnight," she scolded.

"Promise me you'll stay," a voice she didn't recognize resonated in her head, compelling her to remain in the apt.

Shaking her head, Ailsa stepped over the threshold and closed the door. It was time. She had to go.

CHAPTER 11

Ailsa drove her little red Sunfire past the house she'd lived in during the last months of her time in the foster care system. It had been surreal. She'd woken up one morning to find the Blacks had a complete attitude change in how they treated her. She'd been greeted with smiles and hugs when she'd entered the kitchen with the hope of snagging an apple for breakfast. Instead, she'd found herself being led to the kitchen table to join them for a meal of eggs, pancakes, and bacon. In all the time she'd been there, she'd never ate with them at the table. Instead, she'd taken her meals at her relegated spot, standing at the counter. They'd taken her shopping for clothing that didn't come from a thrift store and had actually fit her. Once they'd returned to the house, she'd expected them to drop the pretense that they cared for her and grab the bags of shoes and clothing from her hands, but that hadn't happened. They'd seemed genuinely perplexed as to why she was sleeping in the room behind the kitchen and had insisted she take her things to a room upstairs. Even as she'd enjoyed the feeling of being wanted, she couldn't help waiting for the other shoe to drop. It never did.

Turning off the main road, she drove down a path that was

little more than dirt tracks made by tires that had killed the grass long ago. Slowing her speed so her wheels didn't bottom out in the large divots along the trail, Ailsa pulled off to the side when the copse of trees in came into view.

Clenching her fingers around the steering wheel, she stared out the windshield. Not far from where she parked, stood the grove of trees that always seemed to hold a bit of magick to her. It felt familiar, yet something held her back from going there to explore its mysteries.

Cutting off the gas, Ailsa considered taking her keys with her. Since she didn't have any pockets in her dress, she left them dangling in the ignition, and climbed out. The door closed with a bang loud enough to echo in the air and momentarily startling the wild life to silence.

Ailsa pushed away from the car, only to realize she had fled her apartment without any shoes. "Oh well," she commented to herself, "there's nothing you can do about it now." Stretched up to the middle of her thighs, the long grass obscured the view of where her feet landed. She gave up trying to watch where she walked and crossed her fingers in hope she didn't break an ankle by stepping in a rabbit hole.

With every step she took, Ailsa got closer to her destination and the fog covering her obliterated memories began to thin. The name Kellan popped into her head, followed by a vision of brilliant blue eyes with shards of gold shooting toward dark pupils, the straight line of a regal nose, and full lips she somehow knew had covered every inch of her skin. Lost in the memories flooding her mind, Ailsa didn't realize she not only reached the glen where her relationship with Kellan had first begun, she was standing in the middle of the circle created by the trees. Cocking her head to the side, she heard Kellan's voice telling her to stay out of the glen seven years ago. More recently, it compelled her to stay in her apartment.

Raising a hand, Ailsa closed her fingers around the pendant

Kellan had place around her neck. "What am I doing here?" She had to go. She had to get out here and back to Kellan.

Turning to leave, she gasped. The branches of the trees, reached out to each other, entwining themselves together creating a barrier.

"Leaving so soon?" a feminine voice trilled through the air. It was lovely, light, and musical. It set Ailsa's teeth on edge.

Instinctively, Ailsa tucked her necklace beneath the neckline of her dress. The feel of the wood disc instantly warming against her skin infused her with calm. Taking a deep breath, she plastered a smile on her face before spinning around to face Devany. "It's getting late, and Kellan is waiting for me." She felt some measure of satisfaction at watching the svelte blonde's face flush and her eyes spark with anger.

"He may play with you for awhile, but make no mistake, he will grow bored with you and toss you aside," Devany spewed.

"Like he did you?" Ailsa asked, her voice dripping with mocking sympathy.

"You're not fit to lick his boots."

Ailsa nodded. "Oh, I agree, but as his mate, I am fit to lick every...single...inch of his body. He's quite the feast."

"He is not your mate," Devany screamed.

"Funny. That's not what he told me," Ailsa taunted, trying to keep the woman off balance as she tapped into the magick of the glen with her feet. Apparently, there was a good reason she'd left home shoeless.

They circled each other. Ailsa was acutely aware in the difference in their appearances. While Devany was gold who's allure blazed like the sun, her own coloring was better suited to the softer light of the moon.

"You witless fool." Devany spat. "Do you really think the High Prince of the Fae would really present you, a mongrel of questionable breeding, to the court as his mate?"

"I think Kellan will do whatever he wants."

"Once you're out of the picture, he'll forget all about you. I'll make sure of it."

"Do you think that powder trick you pulled on me will work on him?"

"I won't need it. I'll be there to console him when he discovers you left him."

"Well, I wish I could say it was nice to see you again but really...it hasn't been. Kellan's bringing chocolate croissants home so I need to be going." Giving the crazed woman her back, Ailsa started toward the tree line. She had no doubt the slight would instigate an attack. Although she was nervous, she wasn't scared.

"You. Do. Not. Turn. Your. Back. To. Me." Devany screamed, before an energy ball hit Ailsa in the middle of her back and sent her flying across the field.

Tuck and roll. Tuck and roll, Ailsa thought to herself as the ground rose up to meet her. Flinging out a hand, she pulled on the earth's magick. Instead of hitting hard, the ground softened enough to cushion her fall.

Scrambling to her feet, she threw the same spell at Devany she had previously thrown at Kellan. Only her intent was clear. She wanted to stop Devany. She had to stop her.

Devany released a screech so high in pitch, Ailsa thought her ear drums would burst.

Unwilling to fool herself into thinking she had defeated her opponent, Ailsa closed her eyes and touched her fingers to her mate mark. She located the chord connecting her to Kellan and mentally called out to him.

CHAPTER 12

Pleased the visit with Tess had resulted in her agreeing to return to Faerie long enough for him to present Ailsa at court, Kellan trudged up the three flights of stairs leading to his mate's dwelling. Soon he would have her ensconced in his larger accommodations in Faerie.

He couldn't wait to see Ailsa's face when she found out he had purchase a small tub of the chocolate filling along with her requested croissants. He would have to make sure the cooks became acquainted with the making her favorite pastry.

Midnight's loud yowls reached his ears as he reached the top of the second flight of stairs. Heedless of whether there were mortals watching him through peepholes in their doors or not, Kellan sifted into the kitchen of Ailsa's apartment and set the bag of treats on the breakfast bar.

"Ailsa..." he called out over Midnight's incessant cries.

Bending down, he snatched up the feline by his scruff. "Sàmhach," he commanded. "You are her familiar. Show me what befell her."

Eye to eye with the feline, Kellan received the events of the day from Midnight's memory. "You have served your mistress well," he commended the cat, setting him back on the floor.

Looking to where he saw the card fall from Ailsa's hand, Palm up, her flicked his fingers, raising the stationary from the floor. A touch of magical residue still imbued the missive. He closed his eyes, breaking down the elements of the spell cast on Ailsa. He knew how, and suspecting the where and why, he sent out a telepathic call-to-arms to his guard with the details of where he wanted them to meet him.

Preparing to sift, he felt hard tug on cord connecting his soul to Ailsa and heard her plea for his help. His heart leapt with joy at the knowledge that she had shaken the affects of the memory spell off. He sent her a wave of calm down through their connection along with the message he was coming for her.

∽

*O*utside the glen where he met his destiny, Kellan and his personal guard studied the barrier created by woven tree limbs. He could sense Ailsa's energy but it was muted, their mental link…silent.

As a unit, Kellan and his men raised their arms. Together, they whispered, "fosgailte", as a collective pulse of power flew from their outstretched palms, hitting the barrier. The branches untangled their limbs, granting them entrance into the glade.

"What have you done?" Kellan bellowed, causing Devany to spin unsteadily away from a dome of saplings covering an earthen dais.

"My Prince, you came for me," she whimpered.

Making sure his face did not display the outrage he felt brewing inside, he watched as she stumbled her way to him. He had no desire for her touch, but he would stand that and more to get her away from the bower he suspected contained his mate. Lucky for him Devany paid no attention to the guard at his back.

With a nod of his head, three of them sifted to the sapling vault, while the other two remained with him. He would need them to subdue the crazed female who'd dared to attack his mate. Her gown torn, hair in total disarray, her eyes glowed with madness.

Kellan flinched when she threw her body against his. "What are you doing here, Devany?" Kellan asked, catching her and setting her away from him. "Where is Ailsa?"

"It was awful," she whined.

"I'm sure it was. That doesn't explain why you're here."

"She met me here under false pretenses."

"Did she now? Why?"

Devany stood before him, wringing her hands, "I think she was maybe jealous of the place I have in your life. She told me she was your mate, but I saw that for the lie it was."

His patience was rapidly waning against the growing urge to rush to Ailsa and free her from her prison. Needing to hear what story she was going to spin while he had witnesses, Kellan crossed his arms across his chest and forced his feet to stay planted. "She is Fae, she cannot lie."

Devany's face flushed with fury, "She is a faithless mongrel. She is not Fae."

Kellan felt his self-control slip another notch at her insult to Ailsa. "What did you do?" he bellowed.

"She attacked me. I had to defend myself."

"Did she? Was that before or after you attacked her?" Kellan asked, no longer trying to hide his ire.

"I...I...She had no right to try her paltry spells on me. I am her better."

"She is my chosen mate." He roared. "She is the one I chose, and the one the Goddess saw fit to bless me with."

Devany stared at him in shocked surprise. "No. No. Nooo," she shook her head in denial. "The Goddess hasn't chosen true-mates in centuries. Can't you see? She's devious. She's blinded you with her wiles. She can never be a fit mate to you. I'm the one who should be your mate. We fit so well together. Let me remind you how it used to be between us."

"There was never anything between us, except a roll between the sheets. You knew what to expect when you showed up, uninvited, in my bed. I made myself very clear."

Her fingers curved into claws, Devany flew at him screeching in hysteria. "She can't have you."

With a flick of his hand, stopped her just before her fingernails could rake their way down his face. "Take her and bind her."

The two guards behind him rushed to do his bidding. The hands covered in leather gloves, they yanked Devany's arms behind her, and then slipped iron casings that enclosed her hands and stretched up her arms to her elbows. After which, they clipped them together.

"How did you get past my wards?"

"Do you see how clever I am? I didn't have to get past them. I just needed a mortal to do it for me. I knew with her out of the way, you would see I was perfect for you."

"If you believed Ailsa was an obstacle between us, you couldn't be more wrong. I would never have chosen you to bond with. Never."

"I can't believe you would choose that half-breed nothing over me," she shouted at Kellan as the guards grabbed her upper arms and forced her to her knees.

"Would you like to tell her parents what you think of their most precious child?" Kellan asked, squatting on his hunches.

"Why should I care what they think?"

Kellan rose to his full height. "You should care because they are the High King and Queen Faerie. Ailsa is the daughter who was stolen from them twenty years ago. So you see, Devany, it is you who are not fit to kiss her feet."

Devany laughed maniacally, "You will never have her."

"You will tell me now what you did, or I vow to call the Wild Hunt and demand justice for the injuries you have not only cast upon a Princess of the High Court, but to one who was touched by the Goddess to be a true mate."

At the mention of the Wild Hunt, fear crossed Devany's features for the first time since he entered the glade. Every Fae feared the Huntsman and those who rode with him. "The gu bràth a 'cadal," she whispered, hanging her head in defeat.

Trying to process what she just said, Kellan was aware of the looks the guards exchange with each other. The gu bràth a 'cadal was a forbidden spell. He sifted to the dome beneath which his mate, his heart slept...perhaps never to wake up. The three who guarded Ailsa, discreetly backed away. He hovered his hands over the sapling vault. "I will watch over her now." The branches shivered slowly relinquished their hold on each other and slid back into the ground. The earth had formed a platform on which Ailsa lay. Her hands lay over a blanket of flowers covering her body.

Bending over her, Kellan brushed her silken tresses off her face and peppered her eyelids and cheeks with kisses. "Will you not wake for me, mo chridhe?" Cupping her cheeks, he pressed his brow to hers, "Will you not open your eyes for me?" He hung his head as silence met his questions. Taking a deep breath, he slid his arms beneath Ailsa's neck and the back of her knees. He lifted her to his chest, his heart breaking when her arm flopped limply to the side. His legs felt heavier with every step he took. He'd failed his mate. He'd promised to keep her safe. He failed. He'd promised to save her. He failed.

"Prince Kellan, what should we do with Devany?" one of the guards asked just as he passed the female still on her knees.

"I've summoned the Huntsman."

Devany's screams filled the air. Her apologies and pleas for mercy fell on deaf ears.

"Stay until he gets here. Relay to him all that has transpired here. Then make haste and leave lest you become tempted to join the Hunt." He continued the trek out of the glade. It was time to take his mate home.

CHAPTER 13

She'd lost all sense of time. Ailsa drifted from one shade of darkness to another, with only short glimpses of light to cut through the endless night. At times, she could hear Kellan pleading with her to come back to him. Ailsa tried talking to him through the their link, but her words always bounced back at her like an echo. She would find a way back to her mate. She had to. She couldn't stand hearing the anguish in his voice.

Ailsa squinted her eyes. Light. And it wasn't flickering like fireflies did. It was a cone of light shining from up above. Kellan. Hope surging through her, she ran toward the radiant beam. Laughing with happiness, she came to a stop and frowned. "Kellan?" The response she held her breath to hear was absent. He wasn't there. He hadn't found her.

"*He cannot reach you here,*" a lyrical voice proclaimed.

"Who are you?" Ailsa asked, spinning around trying to locate where the woman speaking to her was. "Where are you?"

"*I am one who would see you restored. I am everywhere.*"

"Can you help me get back to Kellan?"

A bed, draped in white fur, appeared next to her in the circle of light. Wearily she sat on its edge and closed her eyes. She was so tired.

"To get to where you want to be, you must go to where you have already been."

"What does that mean?" she asked impatiently.

"Lay thee down. Take your rest. In your sleep you will find what you seek."

Exhausted and sad, Ailsa laid down on the bed. Her body sighed in relief as the bedding cushioned her tired muscles and her eyes closed. *Just for a minute,* she thought. The touch of a cool hand on her brow both comforted and startled her. Try as she might, Ailsa couldn't convince her eyelids to open.

"Sleep," speaker compelled her. "Dream. Breathe. Wake."

Ailsa wrinkled her nose at the last three words she heard, then knew no more as succumbed to sleep dark embrace.

~

Ailsa's gaze landed on a tall figure standing beneath a tall oak tree greeted. "Kellan..." she whispered into the breeze.

She pressed her fingers to her lips as his head jerked up in surprise. Together, they ran toward one another. Her heart full of joy, Ailsa threw herself into his open arms and wrapped her arms around his neck. Kellan's hug was tight enough she thought she might not draw breath again, but there was no other place she'd rather be.

Kellan set her feet back on the ground. Looking up, she drank in the sight of him. Love and adoration shimmered in his eyes. "I've missed you so much," she confessed.

His mouth closed over hers. Clinging to each other, they kissed with all pent up desperation, love, and hope. Raising her hands, she cupped the sides of his face, and broke the kiss. "We're in the dreaming, aren't we?

Kellan nodded. "Tell me how to find you, mo chridhe," he implored.

"Kellan, I think I'm losing my mind there. It's so dark and cold."

"No," he denied her claim, pulling her tight against him. "Just keep thinking of me…of us. Let me be your light in the dark. I will find a way to wake you, Ailsa."

Dream. Breathe. Wake. The three words she'd heard before she entered the dreaming came unbidden to her mind. Standing before her mate, she now understood what they meant.

"Dream. Breathe. Wake," she repeated the words to Kellan. "Breathe me to life, Kellan," she pleaded as she was pulled away.

"Ailsa…" Kellan cried out to her.

"Breath me to life, my love."

~

Kellan shot of his bed. Heart racing, he turned to look at Ailsa lying peacefully still on the bed. For the first time in weeks, hope bloomed in his heart. They had connected again in the dreaming, and she had given him a clue on how to get her back.

Rounding the foot of the bed, he stared down at her beautiful face. He sat on the side of the mattress wondering if it could really be that simple. Lowering his face to hers, his fingers clasped her chin, and gently pulled it down, parting her lips. "Come back to me, mo chridhe." With all the love he had for her, Kellan took a deep breath. Closing his mouth over hers, Kellan exhaled, filling her lungs with his breath His very essence sought the flickering spark of her soul deep within her, stoking the glowing ember until it flared brightly once more. He sat back up, watching… waiting… hoping.

Her eyelids flying open, Ailsa gasped, "Kellan…"

Clasping her to his chest, Kellan kissed the top of her head, "You came back to me."

"You brought me back, my love, and I never want to be without you again."

"Never again," he agreed, bending his head down to kiss her only to be thwarted by her stomach growling.

"I don't suppose you got those chocolate croissants, did you?"

Kellan booming laughter filled the air as he stood and scooped her up into his arms. "I see I'm going to have to make sure we keep those on hand to make you happy."

Wrapping her arms around his neck, Ailsa shook her head. "Chocolate makes my taste buds and stomach happy, but you... you make me happy."

"And you, gràdh mo chridhe, are the sun and the moon of my world."

Her eyes filled with tears, "Where are you taking me?"

"To introduce you to your parents, the High King and Queen of Faerie." He chuckled at her shocked look. "They never abandoned you, Ailsa. You were taken from them when you were but a child. A strong spell hid your true identity. That's why they couldn't find you."

"But what if they don't like me or want me?"

"How could they not? But if the unthinkable happens, I will never stop wanting you," he declared, kissing her temple.

"I never really put much stock in the fairytales, but you make me believe I can have a Happily Ever After of my own," Ailsa sighed happily, tucking her head in the crook of Kellan's neck. For once, she wasn't biding her time in limbo, she was eagerly looking forward to what the next chapter of her life had in store. After all, it wasn't every day the kiss of Fae Prince brought a girl back to life.

THE END

GAELIC TRANSLATIONS

Mo Molis……..my sweet
gràdh mo chridhe……..love of my heart
Sàmhach……..quiet
Fosgailte……..open
gu bràth a 'cadal……..forever sleeping
mo chridhe……..my heart

ABOUT THE AUTHOR

Author of The Veil Series, Jolanthe Aleksander enjoys writing and reading stories full of romance and a touch of magic. The mother of a son who reminds her to find joy in the simple everyday things, Jolanthe can be found scouring the aisles local books stores, sipping a turtle latte in her favorite coffee shop, or staring out the window…daydreaming. That is, when she isn't reading or writing.

You can follow me here:
Facebook Author Page: www.facebook.com/JolantheAleksander
Eclectic Bard Books: http://eclecticbardbooks.com/category/jolanthes-musings-and-ramblings/
Instagram: https://www.instagram.com/jolanthealeksander/
Twitter: @Joli_Aleksander
Newsletter: http://eepurl.com/djV8gb

AFTERWORD

First Chapter Preview of the first two books in The Veil Series by Jolanthe Aleksander

A Fae King, searching for his lost Queen, finds her in the least likely place...the human realm. He sets himself on a quest not only reclaim his mate, but to restore her memory of who she once was. Should be easy enough for the King of Faerie, right?

BEYOND THE VEIL OF WHISPERED DREAMS

THE VEIL BOOK 1

Things are not always simple or what they seem.
Daria McClaren is content. She has her dance school, her cousin Celine and the man of her dreams. Literally.
Iauron is uneasy. As the High King of the Fae, his chosen Queen Verisiel is calling to him, but he cannot find her. The court insists that she has crossed over. He is not so sure that is the case. He has explored every realm searching. Every realm, but the human one. The race is on. Beyond the veil lie truths waiting to be revealed. Which one will have the courage to look? Will they be in time?

CHAPTER ONE

BEYOND THE VEIL OF WHISPERED DREAMS

The thick fog gave the tall trees an eerie look as the moon's light cast them in shadow. The forest, normally brimming with activity and sounds, was silent. Daria could hear every breath she took, the slight swinging of her arms brushing against the sides of her skirt, and, if asked, she would swear she could hear the blades of grass bending beneath her bare feet. She raised a hand to brush back the damp strands of her dark hair, clinging to the sides of her face and came to a stop.

There they stood, the massive sentries guarding the forest. Two ancient stone megaliths loomed in front of the trees, daring those brave enough to approach to pass over their threshold. The normally quiet stones quietly emitted a low hum that strummed through Daria's body, loosening the knot that was always present in her chest. Of their own volition, her feet carried her over the damp foliage towards the gateway. A tall muscular form appeared between the two stone pillars. Her heart sped up and her breath caught in her chest. He was here. A hand reached out to her. Without thought, she stretched her hand towards the upturned palm waiting for her to grab hold. As their fingertips were a breath away from touching, the fog grew thicker. Panic rose up to

CHAPTER ONE

her throat as she frantically brushed at the fog, searching and reaching for him.

"I will come for you, Verisiel," the low timbre of his voice cutting through the fog seemed further away than the few feet that had separated them. It was a whisper on the wind.

The fog poured in, swirling around her so thick she couldn't see her outstretched hands in front of her. She squealed and spun around when a hand from nowhere landed on her shoulder and shook her.

"Daria. Daria, wake up," the concerned voice of her best friend and cousin, Celine, accompanied the hand gently shaking her shoulder and pulling her from the depths of sleep.

"Wha...what is it?" she asked, brushing her hair out of her face and rubbing the sleep from her eyes.

She watched as Celine walked to the other side of the room and pulled the curtains open, letting the morning light stream into the darkened room. Daria immediately pulled a pillow over her face. There was nothing as annoying in the morning than Celine, who was always chipper and full of energy.

"Your alarm has been going off for a half-hour now. I don't know how you could sleep through it when I could hear it downstairs. It's right next to your head." Hands on her hips, Celine's dark eyes roved over her cousin speculatively, taking in the sheets tangled around Daria's legs. Her eyes twinkled and a smirk curved the corners of her lips. "That must have been some dream. Want to share?" She laughed when the answer to her question came in the form of a pillow flying towards her head. "Fine, be that way, but you better get up or you're going to be late for your morning class."

Daria watched Celine flounce out of her bedroom, her short dark curls bouncing around her head. Her face scrunched up in a scowl at the closing door.

The thought, *'Even her hair is perky in the morning.'* flittered through her mind.

CHAPTER ONE

Groaning, she kicked the tangled sheets off her legs and pondered Celine's question about her dream. Long, slender legs swung off the side of the bed. Dari sat up. Her head hung down and the long dark tresses of hair provided a curtain against the morning light. Eyes closed, she took a deep breath, slowly let it slip past her parted lips, then tried to grab hold of the remnants of her dream. It slipped through her minds fingertips like wisps of smoke, leaving her with only the impression that the man with the blue eyes, who had so often appeared in the dreams she could remember, was there. Cloaked in the shadows.

Daria heard Celine's voice calling to her from downstairs and knew it was time to get a move on or Celine would drink all the coffee. She needed her coffee if being present with a somewhat cheerful façade in her morning class was the goal, but first....a hot shower.

Feeling more awake, Daria pulled back the purple shower curtain and stepped out of the tub. The mist from the shower filled the small space. Despite the heat generated by the water, the tile floor was still cold beneath her feet as she hurried from the rug in front of the tub to the one in front of the sink. A quick swipe at the condensation formed on the mirror revealed the shadows beneath her eyes. They appeared darker due to the fairness of her skin. A touch of makeup was going to be a definite necessity today.

Dressed, ready to face the day, and meet Celine's cheerfulness head on, Daria grabbed her bag sitting atop the chest at the foot of her bed and made her way to the stairs. Hand on the rail Daria paused momentarily. She had a feeling that there was something important that she was forgetting. She checked her bag. All her dance gear was in there as were her e-reader, sunglasses, and the forgotten pamphlet for the renaissance fair that had caught her attention at the gas station. Deciding that the colorful flier was the item she had forgotten about, Daria shook off the lingering feeling that just maybe it was something a little more important

CHAPTER ONE

and skipped down the steps drawn by the rich aroma of coffee wafting up to greet her and lead her by the nose to the kitchen.

The kitchen was filled with sunlight pouring through the bank of windows that framed the semi-circular eating area. Painted in varying shades of yellow and trimmed in white, the kitchen was the heart of their home. Even though neither of them did much in the way of cooking, they had all their serious and not so serious talks there. Daria threw her bag onto the butcher-block island and walked over to the white quartz counter top where the coffee pot sat waiting for her to grab a cup and partake in its heavenly brew.

"It's about time you got down here, " Celine chastised, "I thought for sure I was going to have to call the National Guard in to get you out of bed."

Daria rolled her silvery grey eyes, "Not all of us can be rays of sunshine at the butt crack of dawn."

"Pish posh."

"Before I forget, look at this." Daria slid the pamphlet she pulled from her bag towards Celine, "Think you might want to go? We could dress up."

"Let me look at this while I'm at work and I'll let you know tonight. Speaking of which, let's go ghel or we're both going to be late."

Filling her travel mug, Daria bristled at Celine's use of the Romano term for girl and glared at her cousin.

"Don't give me that look. You have as much gypsy blood in you as I do."

"Not to hear the family tell it. Given a choice, I'd be willing to bet Baba would have tried to talk the family into leaving me in the woods for the beasties to carry off if it wouldn't have gotten them thrown in jail."

"Auntie would never have agreed to that. She loved you more than life itself."

Nodding, Daria swallowed the lump lodged in her throat as

she thought of her mother. She had been gone for three years now, but Daria still choked up at the memory of her mother's unconditional love. Every once in awhile, Daria had caught her mother looking at her quizzically, but the love she held for her could never have been doubted.

"She did, even when she wondered if I were the changeling Baba claimed I was....am."

"Pffft. Baba drank too much and smoked too much. Now grab your stuff and let's go. We're burning daylight."

Daria laughed letting the momentary sadness drift away. Side by side, they walked to their cars, ready to face the day and see what surprises it would bring.

THE VEILED PATH TO DESTINY

THE VEIL BOOK 2

If she had never been at a crossroad before, Daria found herself at one now.

With one foot in the distant past, the other remains firmly entrenched in the present. Daria tries to come to terms with the memories of her previous life as they inundate her mind on an endless loop. Can she deal with the past and find a way to walk the path that is laid out for her future? Is she brave enough to face her destiny, or will she walk away?

Iauron has his Queen back...or does he? He is aware of Daria's lingering doubts about him as she tries to retain her humanity in the face of remembering and accepting who she once was. Though the main threat to her life is temporarily incapacitated, he know it cannot, and will not, remain that way forever.

Not fully Verisiel nor Daria, is she strong enough to meet the coming threat head on? Can she come into her powers and stand by his side? Can he let her go if she cannot accept the whole truth of her situation?

Big questions remain with few answers in sight, and time is running out.

CHAPTER 1

THE VEILED PATH TO DESTINY

    ingers tapping impatiently on her arm, Daria waited to hear the click of the door latching shut. Like a teenager sneaking out at night, she raced to the fireplace. Her fingertips eagerly sought the small, concealed button beneath the mantle that would swing the bookcase away from the wall, allowing her some measure of reprieve from the watching eyes that looked upon her with great expectation.

With bated breath, she waited by the fireplace for the floor to ceiling bookcase to pivot open and reveal the secret passage which would take her to the grotto beneath the castle. Iauron had shown her this hidden oasis with its hot springs only a mere week ago. He had forbidden her, however, from accessing the healing waters on her own, until he had railing installed to ensure safe travel down the winding, damp stone steps.

Slipping through the narrow opening, she made her escape into the dark tunnel. The flickering glow of fire lit the glass-globed sconces, danced along the carved, stone walls as the entrance was once again concealed with the closing of the bookcase. Her hand gripping the stair railing closest to the wall, Daria carefully traipsed down the hand-scraped stone treads. Where one side of the steps was snug against the wall, the other side offered a sheer drop to the ground below. She shuddered with the passing thought that Iauron could have refrained from putting a rail on the other side of the stairs. There was no way on earth she was ever going to use it. Her fear of heights would never allow it, no matter how many safety measures he installed.

Each step down brought her closer to the hovering mist created by the coolness of the cavern ahead and the heat of the water it housed. Wisps of condensation swirled around her as she stepped off the last tread. She was startled when her bare feet landed on a thick carpet instead of the cold floor she was expecting. *He thinks of everything.* She followed the multi-colored, intricately designed swath of plushness through the long tunnel to the domed cavern and the waiting pool.

The closer she got to the entrance of the grotto, the louder the voice of Verisiel, her other self, became in her head. In the two months since the flood gate of memories came crashing down, Verisiel had been a constant presence. Her lyrical voice often offered guidance through the minefield of events that occurred in a time when Daria was but a speck amongst the stardust circling the universe. She was both a comfort and an annoyance.

"You know he will not be pleased you came here on your own."

If he knows me at all, Daria mentally countered, *he'll be expecting me to do exactly that.*

"You willingly risk his wrath."

Do you believe he would hurt me?

"No." Verisiel acquiesced.

Then I risk nothing by being here.

"Yet...."

NO! Daria cut her off, *I will not go back and wait. I may not risk his wrath, but I risk my sanity if I do not find some peace, Verisiel. Surely, even you can understand that.*

"Let me help you, Daria." Verisiel implored. "Fully embrace and accept me, and I will help you."

Daria shook her dark head. *To fully embrace and accept you, I risk you taking over and losing myself.*

"I am already a part of you, Daria."

Yet, I am not part of you, Verisiel. And there lies the difference.

"I do not understand."

I know you don't.

"Will you not reconsider and wait for Iauron?"

No. I won't. Now please, give me the peace I came here for. Just leave me alone with my thoughts and only my thoughts.

Daria could hear Verisiel sigh. "As you wish."

Daria held her breath. As quietly as a whisper against her mind, she felt Verisiel retreat. For the first time in a month, she was alone with her thoughts. It felt foreign as well as freeing. She knew it wouldn't last for long. She had thrown wide the hatch to Verisiel's memories, there was no closing that door once it had been open. She had tried repeatedly to no avail.

For now, she thought as she stepped off the carpet trail onto the smooth, damp, packed down dirt floor, *I'll take whatever break I can get. If that pisses Iauron off, so be it. He'll just have to get over it.*

She took a deep breath and crossed the threshold into the grotto. It was more impressive than she remembered. Firelight from the old-fashioned torches flickered across the surface of gems still embedded in the walls, casting prisms of reds, greens, and blues in a brilliant display. Before her stretched, a whirling pool of water, more a small lake than a pool. Certainly, it was larger than any pool or hot tub she had ever seen.

Her eyes took in the steps into the deep turquoise water. She didn't recall seeing them when Iauron had first brought her here. She had been so stunned by the beauty of the cavern, that even had they been there, she would not have noticed. The domed ceiling gleaming in various shades of gold had Daria wondering how far beneath the castle she was. She shivered at the thought of being so deep underground with nothing but the ceiling to keep the castle from falling down around her.

She tilted her head down then back. Her silver eyes traced over the curve of the dome before her eyelids closed. She took a deep breath, inhaling the sweet clean scent of the water. The warm dampness of the air clung to her skin like morning dew held to the thirsty blades of grass before the sun's blazing heat burned it away. Another deep breath in, she soaked in the energy humming softly through the cavernous space, sensing the protection wards Iauron had put in place.

"I will not leave you unprotected when you seek solace from this new life I have brought you to," he had explained. His large hands had cupped the sides of her face. His blue eyes had sparked with a fire that never failed to draw her into their depths. He was a brilliant flame. She was a moth, all too willing to have her wings singed by the heat of his gaze. Through him, she was reborn again and again.

She pulled back from the memory, yet his presence remained, wrapping her in a cocoon of his warmth, infusing within her body in such a way she knew she would never be alone. She skimmed the surface of her lips with her hand. She could smell him on her skin. Like Pavlov's dogs, or cats as the case may be, she instantly longed to rub her body against his. His kisses were an aphrodisiac, fueling a never satisfied hunger. His touch was a spark that set her body aflame with unquenchable desire. He was her addiction, for which there was no 12-step program to recovery. She fought it, even as she reveled in it.

Lowering her hand, Daria clenched it along with the other one into fists tight enough her fingernails bit into her palms. The pain did nothing to aid her effort to tamp down her raging libido.

She shook her head and unclenched her fists, letting the vestiges of unbridled lust go. Trembling fingers reached up to unfasten the buttons of her top. Daria shivered as the whisper of cool black silk slid from her shoulders, caressed her skin, and pooled at her feet. Her flesh pebbled with goose bumps, Daria stepped out of the puddle created by the shirt she had confiscated from Iauron's wardrobe.

Padding across the short distance to the water's edge, she stared past the hovering, dense mist, to the water's glassy reflection of the cavern's natural luminous décor. Her gaze settled on the middle of the inviting oasis. She placed a hand on the roped railing bracketing the stone slab steps and descended into the warm water. It lapped at her calves, evoking a sigh of pleasure from her open lips. She smiled as the water wrapped around her body the deeper she went.

Shoulder deep, Daria tilted her head back, closed her eyes, inhaled deeply, and lifted her feet up. Gravity took over. She sunk into the clear depths of the deep lake, stretching her body out on the pure white sand when she reached the bottom. She swept her arms through the water to keep herself submerged. Opening her eyes, Daria watched bubbles escaped from her lips and rise to the surface. She wondered at the lack of burning in her oxygen-deprived lungs.

"You are becoming Fae. You need not worry about breathing beneath the water." Verisiel's voice broke her focus to remain at the bottom, precipitating the need to rise as she inhaled water.

Her head clearing the surface, Daria gasped for air as she coughed up the water, clearing her lungs. *You pick waiting until I'm submerged to tell me that?* she asked accusingly.

"You bid me to leave you be."

And yet, here you are. Again.

"Whether you will it or not, Daria, we are a part of one another. Neither of us would be here if it were not for the other. That fact cannot be changed."

Shush. Daria snapped. *You promised to leave me alone with my own thoughts.*

"I did and so I shall," Verisiel agreed, *"I only wished to assure you, you need not worry about drowning."*

Daria sighed sulkily, *Thank you.*

"*You are most welcome. Now, I will leave you to your thoughts.*"

But you'll know what those thoughts are anyway, won't you?

"*It cannot be helped, but I will not intrude.*"

Why is that I get your memories, but can't hear your thoughts?

"*Because you have not fully accepted I am a part of you.*" Verisiel explained resolutely before retreating once again.

And that is the crux of the problem. Well, one of the problems anyway. Daria reflected as she leaned back into the water, floating on the surface.

COMING SOON

CELINE AND COIPEIAL'S STORY

Veiled Hearts Revealed
The Veil Book 3

On a magical island, they came together.
Cóipeáil, the King's shadow, never knew who he was beyond his bond to his Fae father. born and bred to be his master's mirror and guardian, when he was sent to find a human female, he didn't know what it would mean to fall in love with her.
Hidden away on an island thought lost, Celine found paradise with a man she'd never known she wanted.
But love wasn't enough. Not for the bonds of fealty her lover obeyed; not to keep him with her when he doubted his own heart and worth.
Her heart bruised by Cóipeáil's rejection, Celine picked up the pieces of her life and set her course on a new path, determined not to let his absence break her.
But he came back, and all Cóipeáil wants is a chance to rekindle the flame between them and prove that his love for Celine was

COMING SOON

never in question, only his worth for the beautiful woman he wants as his mate.

Will the feelings she's never relinquished for Cóipeáil be enough to bind them back together? Can he convince Celine that even though he left, he's never wanted anyone else?

Is love enough to find a way to bring a human and a Fae together for eternity?

FIND OUT IN: VEILED HEARTS REVEALED~THE VEIL BOOK 3

Made in the USA
Lexington, KY
10 September 2018